dedicated to

marvin's garden

which will bloom forever
in our hearts

Bud

Round the Garden

written by Omri Glaser & illustrated by Byron Glaser & Sandra Higashi

Iris

HARRY N. ABRAMS, INC., PUBLISHERS

This is the tear

that made the puddle

that the sun evaporated

that made the cloud

cirrus

nimbostratus

cumulus

stratus

that made the rain fall

that watered the garden

that made the onion grow

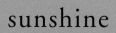

sunshine

carbon dioxide

rain

oxygen

soil

that made the gardeners cry.